Oliver Elephant

Written by Lou Peacock

Illustrated by Helen Stephens

nosy crow

Mummy and Noah and Evie-May Brown
had got up quite early to come into town.
They had lots to do, but they knew where to go –
The Christmassy shop at the end of the row.

"Look, Mummy!" said Noah. "This shop is
so tall! I bet it makes Evie-May feel very small.
But Oliver Elephant's terribly brave."

"Of course," Mummy said,
"and I'm sure he'll behave."

Mummy looked at her list. "Oh, there's so much to find . . .

We need something for Mary –
she's always so kind.

A gift for Aunt Mabel,
and something that's maybe
quite little for Emma –
she's only a baby.

We need something for Chloe
and something for Claire,
and for Great Uncle Jock –
perhaps something to wear.

And Grandma has asked
us to please have a look
for something for Grandad,
who's learning to cook.

There's something else, too –
but, oh, what can it be?"
"I know!" Noah said.
"It's the star for the tree!"

And so they set off,
Mummy leading the way,
past tall rows of shelves
and a pretty display.

While Mummy bought warm gloves
for Great Uncle Jock . . .

Oliver Elephant tried on a sock.

While Mummy found Emma
a tiny toy mouse . . .

Oliver Elephant hid in a house.

While Mummy chose Grandad
Good Cooking For Two . . .

Oliver Elephant played
peek-a-boo.

While Mummy bought lavender
soap for Aunt Mabel . . .

Oliver Elephant danced
on the table.

While Mummy found
Mary an alphabet mug . . .

Oliver Elephant bumped
a glass jug.

And while Mummy bought chocolates for Chloe and Claire . . .

Oliver Elephant slumped on a chair.

"Thank goodness,"
said Mummy,
"we're finally done!
Let's go to the café
and all have a bun."

"Are you hungry?" said Mummy.
"Don't these buns look nice?"
But Noah picked out
a big chocolatey slice!

Then Mummy and Noah
and Evie-May Brown
found somewhere to sit
and they put their things down.

Noah finished his cake.
Mummy put down her cup.
Evie-May was tucked in.
All the bags were picked up.

They put on their coats and were ready to leave . . .

when **suddenly**
Noah tugged hard
at Mum's sleeve.

"Where's Oliver Elephant,
Mummy? Oh no!
We've lost him!
HE'S GONE!

Mummy, where did he go?"

"Oh, Noah," said Mummy, "please, darling, don't cry.

We'll find him in no time. Come on now, let's try."

And so they set off, Noah leading the way,
to check all the places they'd been to that day.

They **rushed** to the chocolate shop
first – just in case.

And **looked** inside vases.
(There **might** have been space.)

They **checked** under tables
piled high with shampoo.

And **peered** behind bookshelves
and customers, too.

They **searched** between teddy bears
lined up in rows.

They **ran** back to menswear
and looked through the clothes.

They searched the whole shop.
They had looked **everywhere**.

**But Oliver Elephant
just wasn't there.**

"Oliver Elephant, where can you be?
Oliver Elephant, come back to me!"

Then, "Wait!" Mummy called out.
"What's wrong, Evie-May?
Quick, Noah, come here!
She's got something to say."

Then Evie-May wriggled and what should appear . . .

but a crumpled blue trunk and a velvety ear?

"My elephant!"
Noah yelled,
spinning him round.

"I thought you were lost!
I'm so happy you're found!"

As Mummy and Noah and Evie-May Brown
were ready to leave Mummy stopped with a frown.

"There's something we've missed – but, oh,
what can it be?"

"I know!" Noah said . . .

..."It's the **star** for the tree."